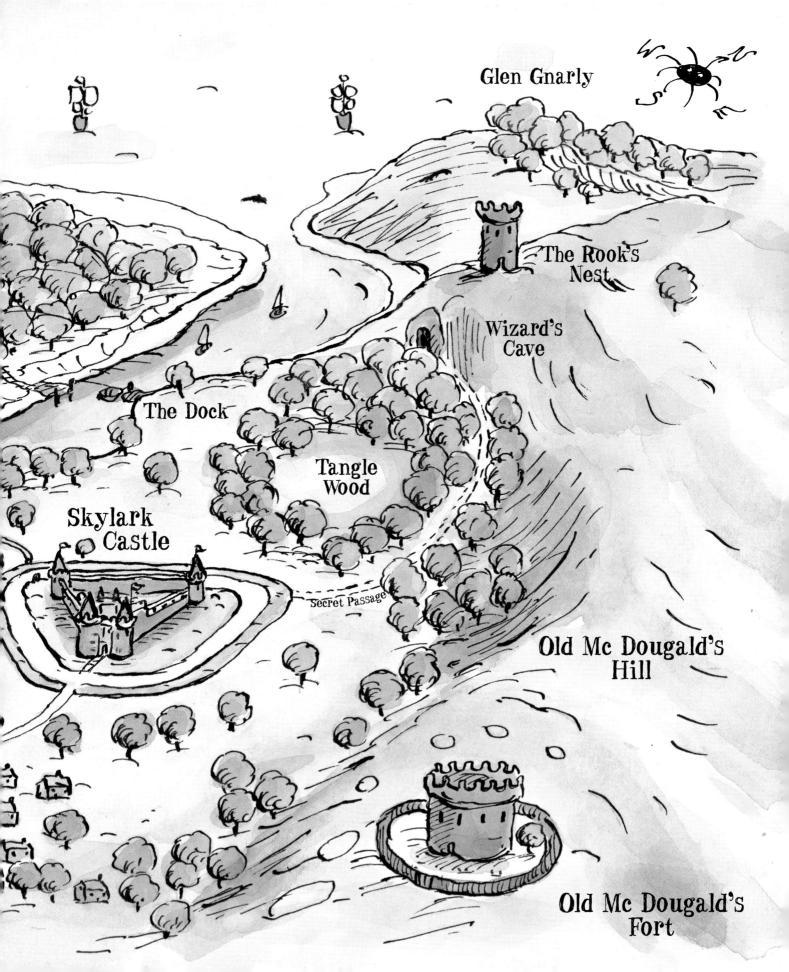

Glen Gnarly

The Rook's
Nest

Wizard's
Cave

The Dock

Tangle
Wood

Skylark
Castle

Secret Passage

Old Mc Dougald's
Hill

Old Mc Dougald's
Fort

PRINCESS LOLA'S WOBBLY WEEK
by Miranda Maxwell-Hyslop

British Library Cataloguing in Publication Data
A catalogue record of this book is available from
the British Library.

ISBN 0 340 87848 7 (HB)
ISBN 0 340 87849 5 (PB)
Copyright © Miranda Maxwell-Hyslop 2005

The right of Miranda Maxwell-Hyslop to be identified as the author
and illustrator of this Work has been asserted by her in
accordance with the Copyright, Designs and Patents Act 1988.

First edition published 2005
10 9 8 7 6 5 4 3 2 1

Published by Hodder Children's Books a division of
Hodder Headline Limited, 338 Euston Road, London NW1 3BH
Printed in China

Princess Lola's
Wobbly Week

To friends, family
and Caerlaverock.

Princess Lola's Wobbly Week

Miranda Maxwell-Hyslop

Hodder Children's Books

A division of Hodder Headline Limited

Princess Lola lives with her friends
in a sparkly castle by the sea.

She has a dog called Dragon who
follows her everywhere.

Because she is a princess...

riding dress

dancing dress

hunting dress

party dress

she always has to wear a dress!

painting dress

bathing dress

ball dress

night dress

But Lola is tired of being
made to wear dresses.
She wants to wear something

DIFFERENT!

She stomps to her room
and thinks.
And then she has an idea.

"If princesses have
to wear dresses," she says,
"then this week
I WON'T BE A PRINCESS!"

So on **Monday**, Lola dresses up as a KNIGHT!

"Hello Princess Lola,"
says Robin.

"I'm NOT Princess Lola, I'm a Knight
in Shining Armour!" Lola thunders.
"Well where is Princess Lola?" says Robin,
and he runs away to look for her.

On **Tuesday**, Lola dresses up as a
PIRATE!

"Hello Princess Lola," says Plop.

"I'm NOT Princess Lola,
I'm a Pirate!" Lola growls.
"Well where is Princess Lola?"
says Plop, and he swims away
to look for her.

On **Wednesday**, Lola dresses up as an OUTLAW!

"Hello Princess Lola,"
says Milly.

"I'm NOT Princess Lola,
I'm an Outlaw!" Lola whispers.
"Well where is Princess Lola?" says Milly,
and she tiptoes away to look for her.

On **Thursday**, Lola feels lonely.

It's fun being a knight, a pirate and an outlaw,
but she really misses her friends.

She sets off to look for them . . .

On **Friday**, she finds them.

"I'm not a crocodile!" roars Plop, "I'm a tiger!"
"I'm not a boy!" storms Robin, "I'm a wizard!"
"I'm not a girl!" sighs Milly, "I'm a fairy!"

"And I am really a PRINCESS!" Lola shouts.

On **Saturday** . . .

Lola minds less
that she has to wear a dress.

And on **Sunday**, she knows whatever she wears . . .

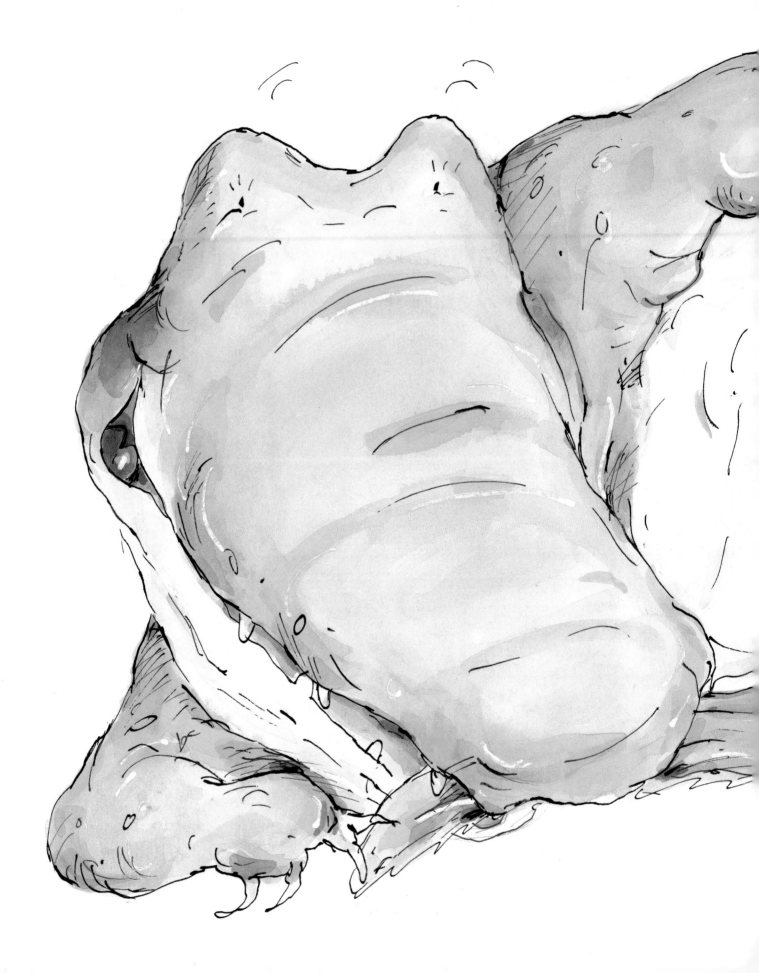

. . . she loves being with her friends

THE BEST!

The Watch

SEA

Hollow
Caves

Deadman's
Harbour

Ravensquick
Forest

The Fishery

The Dribble

The Knights'
Paddock

Battle Hill

To Town

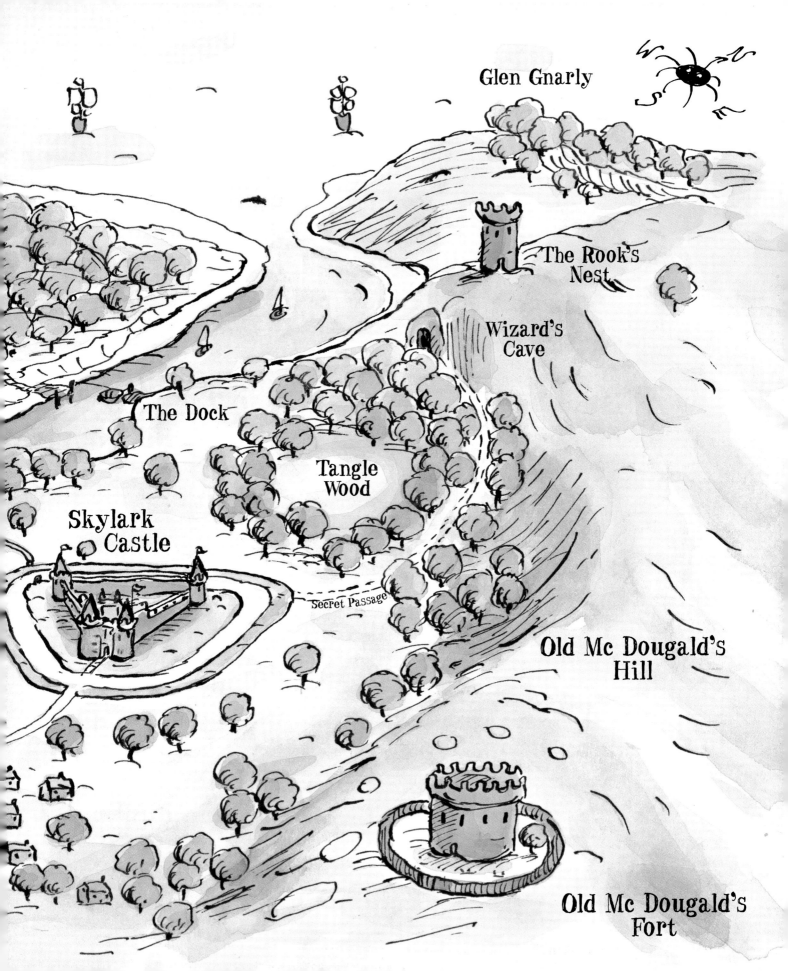

Glen Gnarly

The Rook's
Nest

Wizard's
Cave

The Dock

Tangle
Wood

Skylark
Castle

Secret Passage

Old Mc Dougald's
Hill

Old Mc Dougald's
Fort